DANGEROUS GAMES

STREET WARS

Sue Graves

Rising Stars UK Ltd.
22 Grafton Street, London W1S 4EX
www.risingstars-uk.com

 nasen

NASEN House, 4/5 Amber Business Village, Amber Close,
Amington, Tamworth, Staffordshire B77 4RP

Text © Rising Stars UK Ltd.
The right of Sue Graves to be identified as the author of this work has
been asserted by her in accordance with the Copyright, Design and
Patents Act, 1988.

Published 2009

Cover design: pentacor**big**
Illustrations: Rob Lenihan, So Creative Ltd and Paul Loudon
Text design and typesetting: pentacor**big**
Publisher: Gill Budgell
Editorial project management: Lucy Poddington
Editorial consultant: Lorraine Petersen

British Library Cataloguing in Publication Data.
A CIP record for this book is available from the British Library.

ISBN: 978-1-84680-489-2

Printed by Craft Print International Limited, Singapore

Sima, Kojo and Tom were good mates. They all worked at Dangerous Games, a big computer games company. They had worked there for four years and they loved it. They worked in the same office where they made computer games.

Sima, Kojo and Tom all had different jobs to do. Sima was the designer. She came up with ideas and worked out how the games should look.

Kojo did the technical part. He programmed the games.

Tom tested the computer games and made sure there were no bugs. It was a brilliant job.

Sima, Kojo and Tom liked hanging out after work, too. Sometimes Sima thought of ideas for games when they were hanging out together.

One night they were walking down Penn Street. It was dark and gloomy. The streets were wet.

"I'll be glad to get home," said Sima. She shivered. "I don't like this street. It gives me the creeps."

"Don't be daft," said Tom. "There's no one around."

Kojo crept up behind Sima and jumped at her. Sima yelled.

"Don't be stupid, Kojo," she snapped. "You'll give me a heart attack doing that!"

"It was just a joke," said Kojo. He gave her a hug.

"Yeah, well, it's not funny!" said Sima crossly.

They walked down the street.

Suddenly Kojo spotted something moving in the shadows.

"What's that?" he said. He stood very still and listened.

"Stop it! It's not funny!" said Sima. "You're just trying to spook me."

"I'm not," said Kojo. "Look!"

Coming towards them out of the shadows was a gang of yobs. There were five of them. They were 18 or 19 years old and they looked really mean. They had pulled their hoods up to hide their faces.

The gang was looking for a fight.

"What are you doing on our street?" snarled one of the yobs.

"What do you mean?" said Sima. "It's not your street. We always walk this way home from work."

"Not any more you don't," said another yob. "Not if you want to live, that is!"

He pushed his face closer to Sima's. His breath smelt stale. His eyes looked black and mean.

Sima felt scared. She tugged at Kojo's arm and called out to Tom.

"Run for it!" she yelled.

The three of them ran down the street. They didn't stop running until they got to Sima's flat.

"That was getting scary," said Tom. "I've heard about that gang. Everyone's scared of them. They're always looking for trouble."

But Sima wasn't listening. She was thinking very hard.

Sima took off her coat and sat down.

"Those yobs have given me an idea," she said.

"Go on," said Tom.

"We could make a new computer game called Street Wars," said Sima. "You'd have to get gangs off the streets."

"Nice one," said Tom. He flicked on the TV.

"Let's have a coffee," said Sima. "Then we can work out some ideas for the game."

"Coffee's a good idea," said Tom. "But I don't want to work. I'm watching telly."

"OK," laughed Sima. "I'll work on the game first thing tomorrow."

CHAPTER 2

The next day at the office, Sima set to work to design the game. She worked on a few different ideas. Some of them were good, but some of them were rubbish. She threw the rubbish designs away.

Later she showed her ideas to Kojo. He started to program them that afternoon. A couple of days later, the game was ready. It looked really good.

"Want to test the game?" Sima asked Tom.

Tom sighed. "Those yobs made me so angry," he said. "I wish we could test the game for real."

Sima was puzzled.

"What do you mean, Tom?" she asked.

"I wish we could enter the game," explained Tom. "I wish we could really get those yobs off the streets."

"That's not possible," said Sima. "It's only a game."

"I'm not so sure about that," said Kojo. He thought for a minute or two. "I think if I make one or two changes, we might ... just *might* ..."

"Are you serious?" said Sima.

"No way!" exclaimed Tom.

"Give me some time," said Kojo. "Until then we're taking the long way home!"

Kojo set to work. He hardly spoke to anyone all the next day. Or the day after that. He worked on their game when no one was looking.

"OK, this might just work," he said. It was nearly a week later.

"When shall we test it?" asked Sima.

Kojo looked at his watch. It was almost 5.30 and people were putting on their coats to go home.

"Let's go and have a coffee," he said. "We'll stay behind and wait for everyone to leave the office. Then we'll test the game."

Twenty minutes later, the office was empty.

Kojo clicked on the SW icon on his screen.
The Street Wars game started loading.

"What do we have to do?" asked Sima.

"The game is just as you designed it, Sima,"
explained Kojo. "We have to get the yobs off the
streets. But because we're doing it for real, we
can't use the game controls. We can't use any
weapons, either. We'll have to work out what to
do as things happen."

"Cool!" said Tom.

Then Kojo looked serious.

"I must warn you," he said, "I'm not sure that this has ever been done before. I mean, no one has ever played a game like this for real. We could be in danger. Are you still up for it?"

"Count us in!" said Sima and Tom.

"OK," said Kojo. "We all have to touch the screen at the same time. We'll only know the game is over when we hear the words 'Game over'."

Sima was worried. "Suppose we don't hear the words," she said.

"We've got to hear them. If we don't, we are stuck in the game for ever!" said Kojo. "Are you still up for it?"

"Sure!" said Tom.

"Yeah, me too," said Sima, but she was still worried.

They all put their hands on the screen. A bright light flashed, hurting their eyes. They shut their eyes tight.

CHAPTER 3

Suddenly the three friends felt cold air on their faces. They opened their eyes and looked around. They were standing in Penn Street.

DO YOU THINK THE GAME'S STARTED?

SURE HAS. LOOK!

Coming towards them were the same five yobs they had met before. They looked even bigger and meaner. Like last time, their hoods were pulled over their heads to hide their faces.

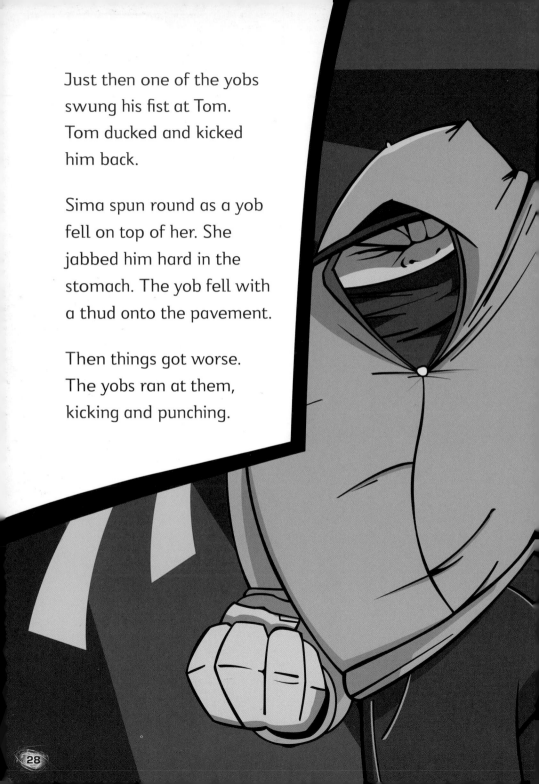

Just then one of the yobs
swung his fist at Tom.
Tom ducked and kicked
him back.

Sima spun round as a yob
fell on top of her. She
jabbed him hard in the
stomach. The yob fell with
a thud onto the pavement.

Then things got worse.
The yobs ran at them,
kicking and punching.

Luckily, at that moment a lorry came down the street. The fight broke up. Kojo, Sima and Tom ran to the top of the street and hid behind some old buildings.

"You're right. This game is way too dangerous," said Sima. "It isn't like a proper computer game where you're safe. We're not safe at all! And we can't win."

"We've got to win," said Kojo. "But we'll have to use our brains."

They sat on the ground and thought hard.

Tom spotted a drain cover.

"I've got an idea," he said. He lifted up the drain cover.

"What are you doing?" asked Sima. "That's a sewer!"

"I know," said Tom. "But sewers are like underground streets. If we use the sewers, we can get under Penn Street where the yobs are. Then we can pick them off a few at a time."

WHAT DO YOU MEAN?

CHAPTER 4

WHAT'S UP?

Tom, Sima and Kojo climbed down into the sewer. It was dark, smelly and wet. Kojo pulled a small torch out of his pocket.

He switched it on and shone it along the sewer tunnel.

They set off down the tunnel. Suddenly Sima screamed.

Kojo shone the torch at Sima. There were rats everywhere. Some were swimming around her feet.

"Ugh, I can't stand rats!" said Kojo. "But they're more scared of us than we are of them. Come on, let's get a move on."

"That makes three of us then," muttered Tom.

They ran on through the sewers.

"Shine the torch up at the ceiling," said Tom.

Kojo shone the torch upwards. There was a drain cover just above them. A small ladder led up to it and a bolt held it in place.

I'M GOING TO CLIMB THE LADDER AND UNBOLT THE COVER. IF THIS WORKS THE YOBS WILL FALL STRAIGHT INTO A TRAP.

Tom climbed up the ladder. He could hear that three of the yobs were further down the street. But two were standing right over the cover.

Tom pointed to the yobs' feet. Kojo and Sima grinned. Tom reached up and quickly tugged the bolt. The yobs yelled as they fell into the sewer.

The yobs sat in the dirty water. They glared at Sima, Kojo and Tom.

"What are you going to do to us?" one of them asked. "Let us out of here, or else!"

"No way!" said Kojo.

Sima took off her scarf. She tied up the yobs. "Don't even think of moving or yelling," she warned.

Sima, Kojo and Tom crept along to the next drain cover. Footsteps were coming closer above their heads. Tom climbed the ladder and pulled the bolt. The drain cover opened and two more yobs fell through, shouting in surprise.

Tom and Kojo pushed them over to the other yobs. They tied them all up together.

ONLY ONE MORE TO GO! THIS IS WORKING WELL.

The three of them went back to the drain cover and Tom climbed the ladder again. The last yob was standing in the middle of the street. He was shouting for his mates.

Tom, Kojo and Sima waited until the yob had his back to the drain cover. Then, very quietly, they crawled out of the drain and stood behind him.

"Keep away from me," said the yob. He backed away.

"You're not so brave without your mates, are you?" said Tom. He moved towards the yob.

The yob looked scared. "Don't hurt me!" he yelled.

"We won't hurt you as long as you never come here again," said Sima.

"No way! Never!" said the yob. He turned and ran for his life.

Sima pointed to the drain. "What shall we do with the others?" she asked.

"They can get themselves out," smiled Kojo.

Suddenly there was a bright light. Sima, Kojo and Tom shut their eyes tightly. A loud voice said, "Game over!"

The light faded and they opened their eyes. They were back in the office. Kojo's computer screen was flashing with the words 'Game over'.

"That was awesome!" said Tom. "But did it really happen or was it only a game?"

Sima put her hand in her pocket and pulled out a yob's baseball cap. She twirled it round and round on her finger.

"It sure was real," she laughed. "And here's the proof."

Kojo grinned, "Nice one, Sima," he said.

"You know what this means guys, don't you?" said Tom.

"What?" asked Kojo.

"We can test other games this way. It's going to be fantastic!" said Tom. He winked at Sima. "That's if you're up for it, Sima!"

Sima grinned. "Bring it on!" she said. "Bring ... it ... *on*!"

GLOSSARY OF TERMS

bug a mistake in a computer program

designer a person who plans how something will work and how it will look

give someone the creeps to scare someone

program to write a computer game or other computer program

sewer an underground passage that carries waste or used water away from buildings

swing a fist to try to punch someone

technical the part of a job which requires special knowledge and skills

Quiz

1 Where do Sima, Tom and Kojo work?

2 Who designs the computer games?

3 Who programs them?

4 Who tests them?

5 What was the name of the street where Sima, Tom and Kojo met the gang?

6 How many yobs were in the gang?

7 What did Tom say sewers were like?

8 What made Sima scream?

9 What did Sima use to tie up the yobs?

10 What proof did Sima have that the game really happened?

ABOUT THE AUTHOR

Sue Graves has taught for thirty years in Cheshire schools. She has been writing for more than ten years and has written well over a hundred books for children and young adults.

"Nearly everyone loves computer games. They are popular with all age groups — especially young adults. But I've often thought it would be amazing to play a computer game for real. To be in on the action would be the best experience ever! That's why I wrote these stories. I hope you enjoy reading them as much as I've enjoyed writing them for you."

ANSWERS TO QUIZ

1 A computer games company called Dangerous Games

2 Sima

3 Kojo

4 Tom

5 Penn Street

6 Five

7 Underground streets

8 Rats in the sewer

9 Her scarf

10 She brought back a yob's baseball cap.